SMELLY SOCKS

To Tina Fabian
Hay River Dene Reserve
Katlodeeche First Nation

The illustrations in this book were painted in watercolor on Arches paper.
Back cover photo of Robert Munsch: Barry Johnston

Text copyright © 2004 by Bob Munsch Enterprises, Ltd.
Illustrations copyright © 2004 by Michael Martchenko.
All rights reserved. Published by Scholastic Inc.
SCHOLASTIC, CARTWHEEL BOOKS, and associated logos
are trademarks and/or registered trademarks of Scholastic Inc.

Library in Congress Cataloging-in-Publication Data available

ISBN 0-439-64948-X

30 29 28 27 26 25 24 23   12 13 14/0
Printed in the U.S.A.   40   • First printing, October 2004

SMELLY SOCKS

BY
ROBERT MUNSCH

ILLUSTRATED BY
MICHAEL MARTCHENKO

Cartwheel ·B·O·O·K·S·®

SCHOLASTIC INC.

New York Toronto London Auckland Sydney
Mexico City New Delhi Hong Kong Buenos Aires

When Tina wanted new socks, her mom took her to the only store in town.

"This store only has black socks," said Tina. "Can we please go across the river and get some really good socks?"

"We can't drive right across the river because there is no bridge here," said Tina's mom. "You know it is a long, long, long way to the only bridge and besides, we don't have a car!"

So Tina went to her grandfather and said, "Can you please take me across the river in your boat? I want to buy some really good socks."

"The motor is not working on the boat," said her grandfather.

"Row!" said Tina. "We can row! I will row and you can sit in the back of the boat."

"You will row?" said her grandfather.

"YES!" said Tina. "Rowing is easy."

So Tina got in the boat and rowed slowly

SPLASH **SPLASH** **SPLASH**

and the boat went in slow circles.

SWISH! *SWISH!* *SWISH!*

Tina rowed fast

SPLASH **SPLASH** **SPLASH** **SPLASH** **SPLASH**

and the boat went in fast circles.

SWISH SWISH SWISH SWISH SWISH!

"This boat has forgotten how to row," said Tina.

"You sit in the back and tell me what to do," said her grandfather.

So Tina sat in the back and told her grandfather how to row, and her grandfather rowed all the way across the river. Then they walked all the way through the town to the big sock store.

At the store Tina tried on socks that were too big, socks that were too little, socks that were too blue, and socks that were too pink.

Tina tried on millions and millions of socks.

Finally she found a perfect pair of red, yellow, and green socks.

Then, since it was almost time for dinner, Tina and her grandfather ran back to the boat, and this time the boat sort of remembered how to row. Tina rowed round and round and round, and still got to the other side.

When they got back, Tina ran home and yelled, "Socks! Socks! Wonderful socks! These are the best socks I have ever seen in my life. Grandpa rowed me all the way across the river to get these socks. I am NEVER going to take them off."

"Never?" said Tina's mother.

"NNNNNNNEVER!" said Tina.

"Uh-oh!" said Tina's mother.

So Tina wore her socks for a long time. She wore them for one, two, three, four, five, six, seven, eight, nine, ten whole days.

Her mother said, "Tina, I know you love these socks. Just let me wash them really quick. They will start to SMELL if you don't get them washed."

"Socks! Socks! Wonderful socks!" said Tina. "I am NEVER, NEVER going to take them off."

After Tina wore her socks for ten more days, the kids at school said, "Tina! What a smell! Change your socks."

"Socks! Wonderful socks!" said Tina. "I am NEVER, NEVER, NEVER, NEVER, NEVER going to take them off."

After Tina wore her socks for ten more days, a whole flock of Canada geese flew over her house and dropped right out of the sky from the smell.

Two moose walked through her yard
and fell over from the smell.
Ducks, raccoons, and squirrels fell
over when she walked to school.

Finally, even a skunk fell over from the smell.

Tina's friends decided to do something. They all came to her house and knocked on the door.

BLAM BLAM BLAM BLAM BLAM!

When Tina opened the door, they grabbed her and carried her to the river. Then they held their noses and took off her socks.

Some of the kids held Tina, and some of the kids washed the socks.

SCRUB SCRUB SCRUB SCRUB SCRUB!

All the fish in the river floated up to the top and acted like they were dead.

The kids washed some more:

SCRUB SCRUB SCRUB SCRUB SCRUB!

All the beavers ran out of the river and went to live with Tina's grandfather.

They washed some more:

SCRUB SCRUB SCRUB SCRUB SCRUB!

Far down the river, people said, "How come the river smells like dirty socks?"

Finally the socks were clean.

"Wow!" said Tina. "They *look* nicer when they are clean.

"Wow!" said Tina. "They *smell* nicer when they are clean.

"Wow!" said Tina. "They *feel* nicer when they are clean."

Tina put on the socks and said, "I am going to wear clean socks from now on."

The beavers left her grandfather's house and went back into the river.

The Canada geese got up off the ground and flew away.

The fish decided that they were not dead after all, and jumped and splashed in the river.

Tina went to her mom and said, "My socks are nice and clean, and I think it would be very nice if you took me to town to get me a nice new red, yellow, and green shirt."

"Promise to wash it?" said her mom.

"No," said Tina. "If I wait long enough, the kids at school will wash it for me."